The Adventures of

Tom Sawyer

Mark Twain

Condensed and Adapted by
W.T. ROBINSON

Illustrated by
RUTH PALMER

Cover Illustrated by
ALBERT SLARK

bendon

The Bendon Junior Classics have been
adapted and illustrated with care and thought
to introduce you to a world of famous authors, characters, ideas,
and great stories that have been loved for generations.

Editor — Kathryn Knight
Creative Director — Gina Rhodes Haynes
And the entire classics project team

THE ADVENTURES OF TOM SAWYER

Copyright © 2017 Bendon, Inc.
Ashland, Ohio 44805 • 1-888-5-BENDON
bendonpub.com

Printed in the United States of America

FOREWORD

A note to the reader—

A classic story rests in your hands. The characters are famous. The tale is timeless.

This Junior Classic edition of *Tom Sawyer* has been carefully condensed and adapted from the original version (which you really *must* read when you're ready for every detail). We kept the well-known phrases for you. We kept Mark Twain's style. And we kept the important imagery and heart of the tale.

Literature is terrific fun! It encourages you to think. It helps you dream. It is full of heroes and villains, suspense and humor, adventure and wonder, and new ideas. It introduces you to writers who reach out across time to say: "Do you want to hear a story I wrote?"

Curl up and enjoy.

CONTENTS

1. Y-o-u-u, Tom – The Thread of a Tale 1

2. Whitewashing – The New Girl 9

3. Huck Finn – Becky Thatcher 25

4. Falling in Love – Failing in Love 37

5. The Graveyard – Murder! 43

6. A Secret Oath – Signed in Blood 53

7. Muff Potter – Pirates – The Island 57

8. Sneaking Ashore – The Funerals 69

9. Taking the Heat – Winning the Heart 83

10. The Murder Trial – Facing Injun Joe 91

11. A Hero – Digging for Hidden Treasure 99

12. Hiding Above – Gold Below 108

13. On Watch – In Room 2 121

14. McDougal's Cave – Huck the Spy 129

15. A Widow Is Saved – A Cave Is Searched 137

16. Lost! – A Light in the Darkness 149

17. Return to the Cave – Under the Cross 161

18. Riches – Rules – Rags – Robbers 171

   About the Author 182

CHARACTERS

TOM SAWYER — a kid full of spunk and mischief who is *not* the model boy of St. Petersburg, Missouri

AUNT POLLY — Tom's Aunt who took him in when his parents died

SID SAWYER — Tom's younger half-brother

COUSIN MARY — Tom's older cousin, Aunt Polly's daughter

HUCKLEBERRY FINN — the young outcast of the village who lives on his own

BECKY THATCHER — the lovely new girl in town who steals Tom's heart

MR. DOBBINS — the strict schoolmaster

Tom's buddies
JEFF THATCHER — Becky's cousin
JIM — the little boy who helps Aunt Polly
BEN ROGERS — the "*Big Missouri* steamboat"
JOE HARPER — a fellow pirate

CHARACTERS

INJUN JOE — a mean, lying villain with revenge on his mind

MUFF POTTER — a foolish ol' man who gets mixed up with Injun Joe

DOCTOR ROBINSON — a young (unfortunate) doctor in town

The pirates of Jackson's Island
THE BLACK AVENGER OF THE SPANISH MAIN
HUCK FINN THE RED-HANDED
THE TERROR OF THE SEAS

THE "SPANIARD" — a mysterious stranger in town… in disguise

THE RAGGED MAN — the Spaniard's partner

THE WELSHMAN, MR. JONES — the old man who lives on Cardiff Hill

JUDGE THATCHER — Becky's father

WIDOW DOUGLAS — the rich old lady whose life is saved by Huck Finn

The Adventures of
Tom Sawyer

CHAPTER ONE

Y-o-u-u, Tom — The Thread of a Tale

"Tom!"

No answer.

"*Tom!*"

No answer.

"What's going on with that boy, I wonder? You, TOM!"

No answer.

"Well, I declare, if I get hold of you I'll—"

The old lady did not finish, for by this time she was bending down and punching under the bed with the broom. She found nothing but the cat. She went to the open door and looked out among the tomato vines and weeds in the garden. No Tom.

"Y-o-u-u, *Tom*!"

There was a slight noise behind her, and she turned just in time to catch a small boy by the back of his jacket and stop his escape.

"There! I might-a thought of that closet. What you been doing in there?"

"Nothing."

"Nothing! Look at your hands. And look at your mouth. What *is* that mess?"

"I don't know, Aunt."

"Well, *I* know. It's jam—that's what it is. Forty times I've said if you didn't let that jam alone I'd wallop you. Hand me that switch."

The switch hung in the air.

"My! Look behind you, Aunt!"

The old lady whirled round and snatched her skirts out of danger. The boy ran in an instant, scrambled up the high board fence, and disappeared over it.

His Aunt Polly stood surprised a moment and then broke into a gentle laugh.

"Hang the boy, can't I never learn anything? Ain't he played enough tricks on me like that by now? He's full of the Old Devil, but he's my own dead sister's boy, poor thing, and I ain't got the heart

to whip him, somehow. I know he'll skip school this afternoon, so I'll just have to make him work tomorrow to punish him. He hates to work on Saturdays more than he hates anything else, and I've *got* to do something or I'll spoil the child."

Tom *did* skip school, and he had a very good time. He got home just in time to help Jim, Auntie's little helper, saw and split the next-day's wood before supper. Tom's younger half-brother, Sid, was already through with his part of the work. (Sid was a quiet boy who never got in much trouble.)

That evening, Tom sat for supper with Sid, Cousin Mary, and Aunt Polly. While Tom was eating, Aunt Polly asked him sly and clever questions—trying to find out if he had skipped out of school that afternoon to go swimming.

"Tom, it was kinda warm in school, warn't it?"

"Yes'm."

"Real warm, warn't it?"

"Yes'm."

"Didn't you want to go swimming, Tom?"

A bit of a scare shot through Tom.

"No'm—well, not very much."

The old lady reached out and felt Tom's shirt. "But you ain't too warm now, though, are you?"

Tom could see what she was up to.

"Some of us pumped water on our heads," he said, "and mine's still wet. See?"

Aunt Polly was upset to think Tom might be fooling her. Then she thought of something...

"Tom, surely you didn't have to undo your shirt collar where I sewed it together, just to pump water on your head, did you?"

Tom felt better. He opened his jacket. His shirt collar was still tightly sewed.

"Bother! Well, go 'long with you," said Aunt Polly. "I thought sure you'd skipped school and been swimming. But I forgive you, Tom. *This* time."

She was half sorry her trick had failed, and half glad that Tom had done the right thing for once.

But Sid said, "Well, now, I thought you sewed his collar with *white* thread, but now it's sewed with *black* thread."

"Why, I did sew it with white! Tom!"

"Siddy, I'll get you for that," shouted Tom, running out the door.

After Tom had scrambled over the back fence, he found a safe place to hide and plan his revenge on Sid. He also had to figure out just how he had messed up on re-sewing his collar.

He looked at the two large needles stuck under the collar of his jacket. One needle had white thread and the other black. Tom wished Aunt Polly would stick to one color or the other. "I can't keep up with 'em," he thought.

He got home pretty late that night. His clothes were dirty and torn from scuffling on the ground. Aunt Polly caught him climbing in his window and knew just the kind of Saturday work she would give him.

CHAPTER TWO

Whitewashing – The New Girl

Saturday morning came. Every child was happy to be out of school for the day—all except Tom.

He appeared on the sidewalk with a bucket of white paint and a long-handled brush. He looked at the fence—thirty yards of high, board fence. He sat down on a tree-box, sad and unhappy.

Jim came skipping along with a tin pail, singing. Bringing water from the town pump had always been hateful work for Tom, but now it did not seem so. He remembered that there were always children at the pump, joking around and trading playthings.

Tom said, "Say, Jim, I'll go get the water if you'll whitewash some."

Jim shook his head. "Can't, Tom. Your Aunt Polly, she tole me I got to go an' git dis water. She say she spec' you would ask me to whitewash, an' so she tole me go 'long an' not to help you—she say *she'd* be boss of de whitewashin'."

"Oh, never you mind what she said, Jim. That's the way she always talks. Gimme the bucket—I won't be gone only a minute. *She* won't ever know."

"Oh, I can't. Ole Miss Polly, she'd whup me good. 'Deed she would."

"*She!* She never spanks anybody hard. She talks awful, but talk don't hurt you much. Jim, I'll give you the most special marble. I'll give you a white alley! It's the finest shootin' marble there is!"

"My! Dat's a mighty fine marble, I tell you! But I'se powerful 'fraid of Miss Polly—"

"And besides, if you'll paint, I'll show you my swollen sore toe. I'll take off the bandage. "

Jim couldn't say no to *this*. He put down his pail, took the marble, and bent over the toe. In another moment he was flying down the street with his pail and a stinging bottom, Tom was busy whitewashing, and Aunt Polly was leaving with a slipper in her hand and victory in her eye.

Tom tried to think of a way out of the mess he was in. Then he got a great idea.

He picked up his brush and went to work. Ben Rogers came in sight, hop-skip-and-jumping, happy as could be. He was eating an apple and giving a long whoo-oop at times, followed by a deep ding-dong-dong, ding-dong-dong—pretending to be the *Big Missouri* river steamboat. He was the boat, captain and engine-bells all at the same time.

"Stop her, sir! Ting-a-ling-ling! Ting-a-ling-ling! Chow! Ch-ch-chow! Chow! Done with the engines, sir! Ting-a-ling-ling! *Shsst, Shsst, Shsst!*" (letting off some steam pressure).

Tom went on whitewashing, paying no attention to Ben, the steamboat. Ben stared a moment and said, "Hi-yi! *You're* in a mess, ain't you!"

No answer. Tom looked at his last paint stroke with the eye of an artist. Tom's mouth watered for the apple, but he stuck to his work.

Ben said, "Hello, old chap, you gotta work, hey?"

Tom turned suddenly.

"Why, it's you, Ben! I hadn't noticed you."

"Say—I'm going in a-swimming, I am. Don't you wish you could? But of course you'd rather *work*—wouldn't you? Course you would!"

Tom studied the boy a bit, and said:

"What do you call work?"

"Why, ain't *that* work?"

"Well, maybe it is, and maybe it ain't. All I know is—it's fun for Tom Sawyer."

"Oh, come, now, you don't mean to say you *like* it?"

The paintbrush kept moving.

"Like it? Well, I don't see why I shouldn't like it. Does a boy get a chance to whitewash a fence every day?"

That changed the way Ben thought about it. He stopped nibbling his apple and began watching Tom closely, getting more and more interested. Soon he said:

"Say, Tom, let *me* whitewash a little."

Tom thought about it and was about to agree, but he changed his mind.

"No—no—I reckon I better not, Ben. You see, Aunt Polly wants this fence done right. I reckon there ain't one boy in a thousand, maybe two thousand, that can do it the way it's got to be done."

"No—is that so? Oh, come, now—lemme just try. Only just a little. Why, I'd let *you*, if you was me, Tom."

"Ben, I'd like to, honest injun, but Aunt Polly—well, Jim wanted to do it, but she wouldn't let him. Won't let Sid, neither. Now don't you see my problem? If you was to try this fence and anything was to happen to it—"

"Oh, shucks, I'll be just as careful. Now lemme try. Say—I'll give you the core of my apple."

"Well, here… No, Ben, I can't. I'm afraid—"

"I'll give you *all* of it!"

Tom gave up the brush, acting like he didn't want to stop painting, but knowing that his plan had worked just right. And while Ben worked and sweated in the sun, Tom sat on a barrel in the shade close by, munched his apple, and planned how he could trap some more kids. He didn't have to wait long. Boys stopped by every little while. They came to laugh at Tom, but stayed to paint the fence.

By the time Ben was tired out, Tom had traded the next chance to Billy Fisher for a kite. When he gave up, Johnny Miller traded for a dead rat and a string to swing it with—and so it went, hour after hour. And when the middle of the afternoon came, Tom was rich, for he also had twelve marbles, part of a harmonica, a piece of blue bottle-glass to look through, a piece of red chalk, a key that wouldn't unlock anything, a tin soldier, a couple of tadpoles, a spool, six firecrackers, a kitten with only one eye, a brass doorknob, a dog collar (but no dog), the handle of a knife, and four pieces of orange peel.

He had fun the whole time, and the fence had three coats of whitewash on it! If he hadn't run out of paint he would have emptied the pockets of every boy in the village.

Tom had figured out that in order to make a man or a boy want something, all you had to do was make the thing hard to get. He thought about his good luck and went back inside the house.

→►◄←

Tom reported to Aunt Polly. "May I go and play now, Aunt?"

"What, already? How much have you done?"

"It's all done, Aunt."

"Tom, don't lie to me."

"I ain't, Aunt. It *is* all done."

Aunt Polly didn't trust Tom. She went out to see for herself. When she found the whole fence whitewashed with three coats, she could hardly believe her eyes.

"Well, there's no getting round it, you can work when you want to, Tom. Go 'long and play, but get back soon, or I'll spank you."

She was so happy with what he had done that she gave him a big red apple and read him a Bible verse about how good it was to work hard for special treats. While her back was turned, Tom snitched a doughnut.

Then Tom skipped out and saw Sid. Soon the air was full of mud balls falling on Sid like a hailstorm, and before Aunt Polly could catch him, Tom was over the fence and gone. He was happy now that he had gotten even with Sid for getting him in trouble over his black thread.

Tom hurried toward town, where the boys were setting up two armies for a battle. Tom was General of one of these armies, Joe Harper was General of the other. Tom's army won a great victory. When the "dead" were counted and all prisoners returned, Tom turned toward home.

As Tom was passing by the house where Jeff Thatcher lived, he saw a girl in the garden—a lovely little blue-eyed girl with long, yellow braids. The great war hero fell without firing a shot.

Who was this new girl? In less than a second he forgot Amy Lawrence, his girlfriend of the past week.

He stared at this new angel secretly, till he was sure she had seen him. Then he pretended he did not know she was there, and began to show off.

While he was in the middle of some cartwheels, he glanced up and saw that the little girl was headed toward the house. Tom came up to the fence, hoping she would stay awhile longer. She stopped a moment on the steps and tossed a pansy over the fence as she went out of sight.

Tom was thrilled!

He slipped over to the flower and picked the pansy up between his bare toes so nobody would notice. Then, hopping off a short distance, he put the pansy inside his jacket. He hung around the fence till sunset, "showing off" as before, and hoping that she was watching him through a window. Finally he went home, with his poor head in a whirl.

All through supper Tom seemed so happy that his aunt wondered what was going on. He took a good scolding for mud-balling Sid, and didn't even seem to care.

CHAPTER THREE

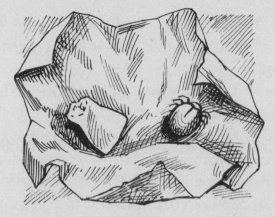

Huck Finn – Becky Thatcher

Monday morning came.

Tom Sawyer was unhappy. Mondays always made him that way—because it began another week's slow suffering in school.

Tom lay thinking. Maybe he could be sick and stay home from school. What could he think of? Suddenly he had an idea. One of his upper front teeth was loose. This was lucky. He began groaning.

Before long, Sid, Cousin Mary, and Aunt Polly were there to see what the trouble was.

"You, Tom! Tom, what's the matter with you?"

"Oh, Auntie, I'm—"

"What's the matter with you, child?"

"Oh, Auntie, it's my tooth!"

"Your tooth, indeed! What's the matter with your tooth?"

"One of them's loose, and it aches awful—just perfectly awful."

"There, there, now, don't begin that groaning again. Open your mouth. Well—your tooth *is* loose, but you're not going to die from that. Mary, get me a chunk of red-hot coal from the fire and a piece of silk thread."

"Oh, please, Auntie, please don't pull it out. It don't hurt any more. I don't want to stay home from school."

"Oh, you don't, don't you? So all this fuss was because you thought you'd get to stay home from school and go a-fishing? Tom, Tom, I love you so, but you seem to try every way you can to break my old heart."

By this time the dental tools were ready. Aunt Polly tied one end of the silk thread round Tom's tooth and tied the other to the bedpost. Then she seized the chunk of fire and suddenly thrust it almost into the boy's face. The tooth was now dangling by the bedpost.

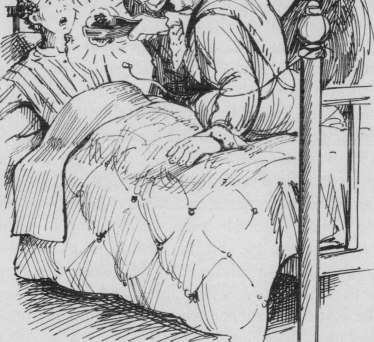

So Tom didn't get out of going to school, but he was able to spit in a new way through the new gap in his teeth. Lots of boys crowded around him on his way to school to get a look at his terrific spitting tricks. Tom thought that even having a tooth pulled could turn out to be a good thing.

Shortly, Tom came upon the young outcast of the village, Huckleberry Finn. Huckleberry had no mother to care for him and was always getting into trouble. All the mothers of St. Petersburg disliked him, but Tom and the other boys wished they had his freedom. Aunt Polly had ordered Tom not to play with Huckleberry, so of course he played with him every chance he got. Huckleberry was always dressed in his Pa's hand-me-down rags. His hat was a mess and his coat hung nearly to the ground. One suspender held up his baggy trousers.

Huckleberry came and went as he pleased. He slept on doorsteps in good weather, and in empty barrels in wet. He did not have to go to school or church. He stayed up late. He went fishing or swimming whenever he wanted, and he was always the first boy to go barefoot in the spring. He never had to wash or put on clean clothes. Every boy in St. Petersburg thought he had a perfect life.

"Hello, Huckleberry!" said Tom.

"Hello yourself, and see how you like it."

"What's that you got?"

"Dead cat."

"Lemme see him, Huck. My, he's pretty stiff. Where'd you get him?"

"Bought him off'n a boy."

"What did you give for it?"

"I give a blue marble that I bought off Ben Rogers for a hoop-stick."

"Say—what is dead cats good for, Huck?"

"Good to get rid of warts."

"How do you do that?"

"Why, you take your cat and go and get in the graveyard around midnight when somebody that was wicked has been buried. When it's midnight, devils will come makin' devil's-fire an' all. When they're taking that dead feller away, you toss your cat after 'em and say, 'Devil follow dead man, cat follow devil, warts follow cat, *I'm* done with you!' That'll get rid of *any* wart."

"Sounds right. Say, Hucky, when you going to try the cat?"

"Tonight. I reckon the devils'll come after old Hoss Williams's body tonight."

"Will ya lemme go with you?"

"Sure—if you ain't scared."

"Scared! 'Tain't likely. Will you *me-yow* like a cat outside my window when you come to get me?"

"Yes—and you me-yow back. Last time, you kep' me a-me-yowing forever."

"I couldn't me-yow that night becuz Auntie was watching me, but I'll me-yow this time, honest. Say—what ya got there?"

"Nothing but a tick bug."

"Where'd you get him?"

"Out in the woods."

"What'll you take for him?"

"I don't know. I don't want to sell him."

"Say, Huck—I'll give you my tooth for him."

"Less see it."

Tom got out a bit of paper and unrolled it.

"Is it real?"

Tom showed him the hole between his teeth.

"Well, all right," said Huckleberry, "it's a trade."

The boys went their own ways, each feeling richer than before.

When Tom reached the little schoolhouse, he walked in quickly as if he had been trying to hurry as fast as he could. The schoolmaster spotted him.

"Thomas Sawyer!"

Tom knew he was in trouble when he heard his full name used.

"Sir!"

"Come up here," said the schoolmaster. "Now, sir, why are you late again, as usual?"

Tom was about to lie, but then he saw the two yellow braids of his latest true love. The new girl was here at school! And right next to her was *the only empty seat* on the girls' side of the schoolhouse. He instantly spoke up.

"I STOPPED TO TALK WITH HUCKLEBERRY FINN!"

The schoolmaster thought the boy had lost his mind. So did the students.

"You—you did *what?*"

"Stopped to talk with Huckleberry Finn."

"Thomas Sawyer, this is the most foolish thing you could have said. Take off your jacket."

The schoolmaster gave Tom a whipping and ordered him to sit with the girls.

This had been Tom's plan all along. He sat down on the pine bench next to the girl with yellow hair.

Before long, Tom had given the girl a peach, drawn some pictures for her, and gotten her interested in him.

"You draw ever so nice—I wish I could draw," said the girl.

"It's easy," whispered Tom. "I'll teach you."

"Oh, will you? When?"

"At noon. Do you go home to eat?"

"I'll stay if you will."

"Good. What's your name?"

"Becky Thatcher. I'm Jeff's cousin. What's your name? Oh, I know. It's Thomas Sawyer."

"That's the name they whip me by. I'm Tom when I'm good. You call me Tom, will you?"

"Yes."

Now Tom began to scrawl some words on his tablet. The girl begged to see what he was writing.

"Oh, it ain't anything," said Tom, but he let her pull his arm away to get a peek.

When Becky saw the words "*I love you*" she said he was a bad boy and hit his hand. But she didn't look too unhappy.

At this point, the schoolmaster grabbed Tom by the ear and marched him back to his own seat. Although Tom's ear tingled, his heart was happy. He had a date with Becky at noon. Tom stared into his book and tried to study.

CHAPTER FOUR

Falling in Love – Failing in Love

Tom couldn't keep his mind on his book. He thought noon would never come—and tried to think of something to make the time go faster. His hand went into his pocket, and his face lit up when he felt the little box that held the tick bug he had gotten from Huck.

Before long, the bug was scampering back and forth on the top of Tom's desk. He and his friend Joe Harper were making a fun game of it. The boys were having a great old time when suddenly a tremendous whack came down on Tom's shoulders, and then another on Joe's. The schoolmaster had been watching—and their fun ended.

When noon finally came, Tom went straight to find Becky Thatcher. In a little while, Tom was teaching Becky to draw, and they began talking.

"Do you love rats?" he asked.

"No! I hate them!"

"Well, I do, too—*live* ones. But I mean *dead* ones, to swing round your head with a string."

"No, I don't care for rats much, either way. What I like is chewing gum," Becky answered.

"Oh, I should say so! I wish I had some now."

"Do you? I've got some. I'll let you chew it awhile, but you must give it back to me."

The two took turns passing the gum back and forth.

"Say, Becky, was you ever engaged?" asked Tom.

"What's that?"

"Why, engaged to be married."

"No."

"Would you like to?"

"I reckon so. I don't know. What is it like?"

"Like? Why it ain't like anything. You only just tell a boy you won't ever like anybody but him, ever, ever, ever. And then you kiss, and that's all. Anybody can do it."

Before long they were "engaged."

"Oh, it's so nice. I never heard of it before," said Becky.

"Oh, it's ever so fun!" agreed Tom. "Why, me and Amy Lawrence—"

Becky's big eyes told Tom that he had just made a big mistake.

"Oh, Tom! Then I ain't the first you've ever been engaged to!" she said, starting to cry.

"Oh, don't cry, Becky. I don't care for her anymore."

"Yes, you do, Tom—you know you do."

"Becky, I—I don't care for anybody but you."

No reply. Just sobs.

Tom got out his favorite treasure, a brass knob, and tried to give it to her to make up for his awful mistake.

"Please, Becky, won't you take it?"

She threw it to the floor. Tom left the school and decided not to come back for the rest of the day. Becky watched him disappear.

"Tom! Come back, Tom!"

She listened, but there was no answer. Her heart was broken.

Tom wandered around for a while, trying to think what he could do now to forget Becky. Should he run away? Should he become a clown in a circus? Or maybe he should become a soldier and a hero. No—better still, he would join the Indians and hunt buffaloes.

But no, there was something even better than this. He would be a pirate! That was it! How his name would make people shudder! He would sail the dancing seas in his black ship! And then he would suddenly appear in Sunday school in his black velvet coat, his great boots, his red sash, his great feathered hat, and his cutlass at his side! He would wave his flag with the skull and crossbones on it and hear the people whisper, "It's Tom Sawyer the Pirate!—the Black Avenger of the Spanish Main!"

Yes, that's what he would do! He would run away from home and start his new life the very next morning!

CHAPTER FIVE

The Graveyard – Murder!

Tom lay awake that night and waited for Huck's signal. The clock struck ten and then eleven. Finally, he heard a faint me-yow. He me-yow'd back as he climbed out his bedroom window and jumped to the ground. Huckleberry Finn was there—with his dead cat.

Before long, they were crawling through the high grass of the dark graveyard. A faint wind moaned through the trees. They found the new grave they were looking for, and hid under some elm trees. An owl hooted somewhere in the night.

"Say, Hucky—do you reckon old dead Hoss Williams hears us talking?" Tom whispered.

"O' course he does. Least his spirit does."

It was silent again for a time. Then Tom grabbed Huck's arm.

"Sh!"

"What is it, Tom?"

"Sh! There 'tis again! Didn't you hear it?"

"I—"

"There! Now you hear it?"

"Lord, Tom, they're coming! They're coming, sure. What'll we do?"

"I dunno. Think they'll see us?"

"Oh, Tom, them devils can see in the dark, same as cats. I wisht I hadn't come."

"Oh, don't be scared. If we keep perfectly still, maybe they won't notice us at all."

"I'll try to, Tom, but, Lord, I'm all shaky."

"Listen!"

The boys bent their heads together and hardly breathed. A faint sound of voices floated up from the far end of the graveyard.

"Look! See there!" whispered Tom. "What is it?"

"It's devil-fire. Oh, Tom, this is awful."

Some shadows came near—shadows swinging a tin lantern.

Huckleberry whispered with a shudder, "It's the devils sure enough. Three of 'em! Lordy, Tom, we're goners! Can you pray?"

"I'll try, but don't you worry. They ain't going to hurt us… Now I lay me down to sleep, I—"

"Sh!"

"What is it, Huck?"

"They're *humans!* One of 'em is ol' Muff Potter."

"No—'tain't so, is it?"

"Don't you move. He sounds like he's on the whiskey. He might not notice us."

"All right, I'll keep still. Say, Huck, I know another one of them voices. It's Injun Joe."

"That's so—that murderin' half-breed! I'd be happier if they *was* devils. What kin they be up to?"

The whispering stopped now, for the three men had reached the grave and stood within a few feet of the boys' hiding spot.

"Here it is," said a third voice.

The boys looked at each other in wonder—it was the voice of young Doctor Robinson! *He must be after a body for his medical studies.*

Potter and Injun Joe had a wheelbarrow with a rope and a couple of shovels on it. Soon they were digging up the grave. Finally a spade struck upon the coffin, and the men lifted it out onto the ground. They pried off the lid, got out the body and tied it on the wheelbarrow.

Potter took out a large knife, cut off the dangling end of the rope, and said, "Now the thing's ready, Doc, and you'll just pay another five dollars, or here it stays."

"That's the talk!" said Injun Joe.

"Look here, what does this mean?" said the doctor. "I've already paid you."

"Yes, and you done more than that," said Injun Joe. "Five years ago you drove me away from your father's kitchen one night, when I come to ask for something to eat. When I swore I'd get even with you if it took a hundred years, your father had me jailed. Did you think I'd forget? And now I've *got* you, and you got to settle up!"

He was threatening the doctor, with his fist in his face. The doctor struck out suddenly and put Injun Joe on the ground. Potter dropped his knife and exclaimed:

"Here, now, don't you hit my pard!"

In the next moment, Muff Potter had grabbed the doctor and the two were struggling. Injun Joe sprang to his feet, his eyes flaming. He snatched up Potter's knife, and went creeping, catlike and slinking, round and round the men. All at once the doctor got himself free, picked up the heavy headboard of Williams's grave, and knocked Potter to the ground with it—and in the same instant the Indian saw his chance and drove the knife into the young doctor's chest. Doctor Robinson staggered and fell on Muff Potter, dripping blood all over him. At that, the two frightened boys went running away in the dark.

Injun Joe stood over the two men. The doctor was dead.

"*That* score is settled—curse you," he muttered.

Then Injun Joe looked at Muff Potter and saw that he had been knocked out cold. He laid the knife in Potter's open right hand, and sat down on the coffin.

Potter began to stir and moan. His hand closed around the knife. He held it up, looked at it, and let it fall with a shudder. Then he sat up, pushing the body from him, not knowing what was going on.

"Lord, what's this, Joe?" he said.

"It's a dirty business," said Joe, without moving.

"What did you do it for, Joe?" asked Potter.

"I? I never done it! *You* done it, Muff Potter! You two was fighting, and he hit you with the headboard and you fell flat. Then you staggered up and shoved the knife in him."

"Oh, I don't remember a thing. It was all because of the whiskey, I reckon. Say you won't tell, Joe. You won't tell, *will* you, Joe?"

"No, I won't squeal on you."

"Oh, Joe, you're an angel." Potter began to cry.

"Come, now, that's enough of that. Let's get out of here. You go one way and I'll go another."

Potter started running. Injun Joe stood looking after him and thinking.

"If he's as confused from the crack on the head and the whiskey as I think he is, he'll forget his knife is still here."

Two or three minutes later, the only things left in the graveyard were the murdered man, the dug-up body of Hoss Williams, the coffin, the open grave—and Muff Potter's knife.

CHAPTER SIX

A Secret Oath – Signed in Blood

The two boys ran on and on toward the village, scared to death. At last, they burst through the door of an old empty building and fell exhausted on the floor.

"Huck, what do you suppose will happen?"

"If Doctor Robinson dies, I reckon there'll be a hanging."

Tom was thinking. "Who'll tell who done it? Us?"

"What are you talking about? S'pose something happened and Injun Joe didn't hang? Why, if we told, he'd kill us for sure. If anybody tells, let Muff Potter do it, if he's fool enough."

Tom said nothing—just went on thinking.

Presently Tom whispered, "Huck, Muff Potter don't know it. He'd just got that whack on the head when Injun Joe done it. He won't remember anything about it."

"By golly, that's so, Tom!"

"Hucky, you sure you can keep mum about what we seen?"

"Tom, we *got* to keep quiet. That devil Injun Joe would kill us for sure if we was to squeal 'bout this. Now, lookyhere, Tom, let's take hands and swear to one another—that's what we got to do—swear to each other that we'll never say a word."

"I'm agreed. It's the best thing. Should we just hold hands and swear that we—"

"Oh, no, that wouldn't do for this," said Huck. "There should be something in writing 'bout a big thing like this—a secret oath—signed in blood."

With that, Tom wrote out some fine words in red chalk on a piece of pine bark.

Then Tom took a needle from his jacket. Both boys pricked their thumbs and signed their initials in blood. They buried the bark and swore again to one another that they would never, ever tell a thing about what had gone on in the graveyard. Their lips were sealed!

Huck Finn and Tom Sawyer swears they will keep mum about this and they wish they may drop down dead in their tracks if they ever tell and they rot.

TS HF

Tom crawled through his bedroom window and undressed as quietly as he could. He didn't know that Sid was still awake.

The next morning started out badly for Tom. Sid had told Aunt Polly that Tom had sneaked in late, and she was upset. Then, when Tom got to school, he got a whipping for skipping school the day before. And to make things even worse, Tom found something wrapped in paper on his desk. It was the brass knob he had given Becky. His heart was broken.

CHAPTER SEVEN

Muff Potter – Pirates – The Island

By noon that day, the whole village of St. Petersburg knew that Doctor Robinson had been killed with Muff Potter's knife. Everyone said that Muff Potter should be hung if they caught him.

All the villagers began to make their way to the graveyard. Tom and Huck were among them. Tom shivered from head to toe when he saw Injun Joe in the crowd.

As the Sheriff appeared over the hill leading someone, the people began shouting, "It's him! It's Muff Potter!"

The Sheriff came through the crowd with Muff Potter by the arm.

Muff's face and eyes showed his fear. When the poor fellow stood before the murdered man, he began shaking. He put his face in his hands and burst into tears.

"I didn't do it, friends," he sobbed. "Upon my word and honor, I never done it." Then he saw Injun Joe in the crowd. "Oh, Injun Joe, you promised me you'd never—"

"Is this your knife?" said the Sheriff, holding it in front of Muff.

Potter would have fallen if the crowd had not held him. He shuddered and hung his head as if he had given up.

"Tell 'em, Joe," Muff begged. "Tell 'em. It ain't any use anymore."

Huckleberry and Tom stood speechless as they heard Injun Joe lie about what had gone on. When they heard him say that Muff had done the killing, the boys wanted to break their oath and save poor innocent Muff. But they said nothing, not even when Injun Joe repeated the same lie at the courthouse, under oath.

Tom did not sleep well for the whole next week. His fear of Injun Joe and his guilt about keeping the awful secret were driving him crazy.

Every day or two, Tom went to the little jail-window and smuggled small treats through to Muff. This seemed to help his guilty feelings.

Tom began to feel sorry for himself after a while. He couldn't tell anyone his secret, and even his new girlfriend was mad at him. What was he to do? Then it came to him. Yes, they had forced him to it at last—he would lead the life of crime that he had thought about a week before, as a pirate on the high seas.

It just so happened that Tom's friend, Joe Harper, was ready to do something different, too. He had just gotten a beating from his mother for drinking some cream—and he hadn't even *tasted* it. So, when the two boys met, they were both ready to run away and find a new life.

Joe was for being a hermit and living on food scraps in a hidden cave. But after listening to Tom, he decided that it would be a lot more fun to be a pirate. The two pirates hunted up Huckleberry Finn, who agreed to join them.

First, they needed a hideout. They all agreed on Jackson's Island, since nobody lived there and it was only three miles down the Mississippi River from St. Petersburg. It was a small, wooded island that rose out of the water where the river was only about a mile wide. It lay just a swim away from the Illinois side. It was too far to swim to from their own Missouri side, but they could reach it by riding the current on a raft.

The three new pirates made plans to meet at midnight at a place on the riverbank above St. Petersburg where they knew a small log raft was kept. They aimed to capture the log raft and begin their life of crime on the high seas. Who would be their first victims, they didn't know.

About midnight, Tom arrived with a boiled ham and a few other things. Tom listened a moment, but heard not a sound. Then he gave a low whistle. From somewhere below, a cautious voice said:

"Who goes there?"

"Tom Sawyer, the Black Avenger of the Spanish Main. Name your names."

"Huck Finn the Red-Handed, and Joe Harper the Terror of the Seas." Tom had come up with these names from some of his favorite stories.

"All is well. Give the password."

Two hoarse whispers delivered the same awful word:

"Blood!"

The Terror of the Seas had brought a slab of bacon. Finn the Red-Handed had stolen a frying pan. The Black Avenger of the Spanish Main said it would never do to start without some fire. So, they helped themselves to a live coal left over from the fire of some campers who had gone off to town.

They shoved off on the little raft. Tom shouted out orders to the crew which none of them understood, including Tom. But they sounded real "pirate-like" and important.

"Luff, and bring her to the wind!"

"Aye-aye, sir!"

"Steady, steady-y-y-y!"

"Steady it is, sir!"

"Let her go off a point!"

"Point it is, sir!"

"Up the mainsail! Down the jigsa'll! Port the mizz'nmast 'round to starboard, me mates!"

After Tom ran out of make-believe orders, the crew quieted down and the raft floated on down the Mississippi. Soon they were passing in front of St. Petersburg. Tom wished Becky could see him now, facing death on the wild seas.

About two o'clock in the morning they reached the sandy shore of Jackson's Island. They waded back and forth, carrying their things to land. There was part of an old sail on the little raft, and this they spread as a tent to cover their food. But they would sleep in the open air in good weather, for this is what outlaws did.

They made a fire using the live coal they had brought. After a supper of bacon, the boys stretched themselves out on the grass, filled with happiness.

"Ain't it great?" said Joe.

"It's *wild*," said Tom. "What would the boys say if they could see us?"

"Say? Well, they'd just die to be here—hey, Hucky?"

"I reckon so," said Huckleberry. "Anyways, I'm happy. I don't want nothing better'n this."

"It's just the life for me," said Tom. "You don't have go to school, and wash, and all that foolishness."

Gradually the talk stopped, and the little pirates got sleepy. The corncob pipe dropped from the fingers of the Red-Handed. The Terror of the Seas and the Black Avenger of the Spanish Main said their prayers to themselves, and within minutes, all three were sound asleep.

Tom woke the other pirates in the morning, and in a minute or two they had their clothes off and were splashing in the river. When they got back to camp, Joe sliced some bacon for breakfast while Tom and Huck caught a few small fish. They fried the fish with the bacon. No breakfast had ever tasted better.

They went off through the woods to do some exploring. It was late afternoon when they got back to camp and sat down in the shade to talk. But the talk soon died out, and they all began thinking quietly to themselves. Each of them was feeling homesick, but they were ashamed to say so. All of a sudden, they heard a large boom in the distance.

"What is it?!" cried Joe.

"Hush!" said Tom. "Listen."

The same boom came again.

They sprang to their feet and hurried to the shore for a look. The little steam ferryboat was about a mile below St. Petersburg, her deck crowded with people. Suddenly, a great puff of white smoke burst from the ferryboat's side, and the same boom sounded again.

"I know now!" exclaimed Tom. "Somebody's drownded! They're lookin' for him in the river."

"That's it!" said Huck. "They shoot a cannon over the water to make the body rise."

"By jings, I wish I was over there now," said Joe.

"I do, too," said Huck. "I'd give heaps to know who it is."

Tom was thinking hard. "Boys," he said, "I know who's drownded—it's *us!*"

They felt like heroes in an instant. People might even be feeling sorry for the times they had been unkind to them. It was great to be a pirate, after all.

As evening came, the boats stopped searching, and the pirates returned to camp. When darkness came, they stopped talking and gazed into the fire. The excitement was gone now, and Joe could not help but think of the people at home who might be sad and worried. He asked what the others thought about going back home. Tom made fun of him, and Huck went along with Tom.

That night, when the others were asleep, Tom left the boys a note on some sycamore bark. He wrote another note, which he rolled up and stuck in his pocket. Then he secretly tiptoed through the trees toward the river.

CHAPTER EIGHT

Sneaking Ashore – The Funerals

Tom knew he couldn't steer the raft upstream against the current. So he began wading the shallow waters that led to the Illinois side. He swam the remaining hundred yards to shore, and then hiked his way north. Shortly before ten o'clock, he reached the Illinois ferrylanding that lay just across from St. Petersburg, Missouri. He saw the ferryboat lying in the shadow of the trees and the high bank.

Good! he thought. *It hasn't left yet for its final crossing of the night.*

Everything was silent under the blinking stars. Tom slipped quietly into the little skiff tied to the ferryboat's side and hid there during the crossing.

When the ferryboat pulled up to the dock near St. Petersburg, Tom slid into the water and swam to shore. Then he ran along the back streets of the village, and soon found himself at his aunt's back fence. He climbed over and peeked through a window into Aunt Polly's bedroom. There sat Aunt Polly, Sid, Mary, and Joe Harper's mother, talking. They were by the bed, and the bed was between them and the door. Tom cracked open the door and was able to slip into the room and crawl under the bed without being seen.

"He warn't *bad*—only mischievous," Aunt Polly was saying. "And he was the best-hearted boy that ever was"—and she began to cry.

"It was just the same with my Joe," said Mrs. Harper. "He was full of his devilment, but he was just as unselfish and kind as he could be. Lordy me, to think I went and whipped him for taking that cream, never once remembering that I had thrown it out myself because it was sour." Mrs. Harper cried as if her heart would break.

"Oh, Mrs. Harper, I don't know how to give him up!" cried Aunt Polly.

Soon Tom was crying, too—feeling mighty sorry for himself.

Tom went on listening and found out that everyone believed the boys might have drowned in the river. This was Wednesday night. If the bodies were still missing on Sunday, the village would hold the boys' funerals. Tom shivered.

Finally, Mrs. Harper left, sobbing. Sid and Mary went off to bed.

Aunt Polly knelt down and prayed for Tom with so much love that he was soon crying his eyes out again.

When Aunt Polly was asleep, Tom slipped from under the bed and stood looking at her. He was going to leave the note he had written, but then a more exciting idea came to him. He put the note back into his pocket, gave his sweet Auntie a light kiss, and then sneaked out the door.

Tom made his way back to the ferrylanding. He untied the little skiff from the ferryboat, paddled his way across the river and left the skiff at the Illinois-side ferrylanding. He had half a mind to keep the skiff, since he was a pirate, but he knew there'd be a search for it. Instead he hiked back down the wooded Illinois shoreline, swam across to the island, and waded to shore.

He sat down and took a long rest just outside the camp. When the sun was coming up, he crept in close and could hear Joe and Huck talking.

"No, Tom's true-blue, Huck, and he'll come back. He won't leave us. He knows that would be a disgrace to a pirate. He's up to something. His note says if he ain't back by morning, to go ahead and have breakfast."

"And here he is!" shouted Tom, jumping out of the bushes.

After a big breakfast of bacon and fish, Tom told his story. They all felt like proud heroes when they knew how much they were missed.

The three pirates had an exciting time over the next couple of days, but thoughts of home kept coming back to them. Tom even found himself writing "*Becky*" in the sand with his big toe.

By now, Joe was so homesick that he could hardly stand it. Huck was sad, too. Tom felt the same way, but tried hard not to show it. He had a plan that he wanted to keep a secret for now, but if things didn't cheer up, he might have to tell them soon. He tried to brighten Joe and Huck up with the idea of a treasure hunt.

"I bet there's been pirates on this island before, boys. How'd you feel about finding a rotten chest full of gold and silver—hey?"

But the two boys showed little interest. Joe sat poking the sand with a stick, looking very gloomy.

"Oh, boys," said Joe, "let's give it up. I want to go home. It's so lonesome."

"Oh, no, Joe. You'll feel better before long," said Tom. "Just think of the fishing and swimming that's here."

"They ain't no good. I don't seem to care for things, somehow, when there ain't anybody to tell me I can't do 'em. I want to go home," said Joe, and began packing his things.

"I want to go, too, Tom," said Huck.

"Well, go 'long—who's holdin' you back?"

Huck took his clothes and started off with Joe.

Tom stood looking after him, thinking. All at once, he ran yelling after his friends.

"Wait! Wait! I want to tell you something!"

They stopped, and Tom let them in on his secret plan. As soon as they heard it, they let out a whoop of joy. The boys came happily back and began their games again, chattering all the time about Tom's neat plan.

Around midnight, the worst thunderstorm the boys had ever seen ripped through the camp. The thunder was like an army of cannons, and the lightning made the woods as bright as day. The wind tore away their little sail-tent, and the terrified boys fled through the rain to a great oak near the riverbank. Here they huddled, shivering from the cold and the exploding thunder. Trees crashed to the ground. The river drenched them in its wild spray. It only lasted about thirty minutes, but it seemed like hours to the three brave pirates. At last, things quieted down, and they dropped off into a wet, exhausted sleep.

Whether it was the storm or what, Tom didn't know, but the next morning he saw that Joe and Huck were homesick again. Tom tried to cheer them up and got them interested in playing Indians. It wasn't long before they were stripped to their shorts and striped from head to toe with black mud. The three Indians, all chiefs of course, went tearing off through the woods to attack an English village.

We will leave them for now to laugh and brag and count their captives.

There was no laughing in the little village that same Saturday afternoon. St. Petersburg was strangely quiet. Mrs. Harper and Aunt Polly both cried themselves to sleep that night as they thought about the next day.

The little church was full Sunday morning for the funerals of the three boys. The minister spread his hands and prayed. A moving hymn was sung, and the Bible verse followed:

"I am the Resurrection and the Life."

A moment later, the church door creaked. The minister raised his crying eyes and could not believe what he saw. All at once, everyone in the church stood and stared while the three *dead* boys came marching in. They had been hiding in back, listening to their own funeral sermon!

Aunt Polly, Mary, and the Harpers hugged and kissed their boys, while poor Huck stood alone. He started to sneak away, but Tom grabbed him.

"Aunt Polly, it ain't fair. Somebody's got to be glad to see Huck."

"You're right, Tom," said his aunt. "I'm glad to see him, poor motherless thing!" And the loving hugs that Aunt Polly gave him made Huck feel even worse than he had before.

Everybody began to sing thanks to God. It shook the whole church. Tom Sawyer the Pirate looked around and noticed how the other children looked up to him in admiration. This was the proudest moment of his life.

Tom got more spanks and kisses that day—depending on how Aunt Polly felt at the time—than he had gotten before in a year.

CHAPTER NINE

Taking the Heat–Winning the Heart

'That had been Tom's great secret—the plan to return home with his brother pirates and attend their own funerals. They had paddled over to the Missouri shore on their log raft and landed five or six miles below St. Petersburg. They had slept in the woods at the edge of the village the night before, and then sneaked into a room at the back of the church early Sunday morning.

What a hero Tom was now! At school the next day, the children made so much of Tom and Joe that the two heroes became "stuck-up." They began to tell their adventures—and the more they told, the more they made up and added to the story.

Tom decided that he no longer needed to chase after Becky Thatcher. Now that he was a hero, maybe she'd want to "make up." When Becky arrived at school, Tom pretended not to see her. Before long, Becky started watching Tom out of the corner of her eye and noticed that he was talking more to Amy Lawrence than anyone else. She was jealous and a little angry. She got closer to Tom and began speaking loudly to one of the girls.

"Why, Mary Austin, I'm glad to see you. I wanted to tell you about my picnic."

"Oh, that's jolly. When is it going to be?"

"In a little while. Maybe around vacation time."

"Oh, won't it be fun! You going to have all the girls and boys?"

"Yes, everyone that's friends to me—or wants to be." She sneaked a peek at Tom, but he kept on talking to Amy Lawrence.

Soon all the children were begging to come to the picnic, except Tom and Amy. Tom turned coolly away, and took Amy with him.

Tears came to Becky's eyes.

Tom ran home at noon. He could not take any more. How could Becky stay so mad at him? Why was *he* acting so mean, too?

He returned to school after lunch with a heavy heart—until he was lucky enough to spot Becky Thatcher on the way. He ran to her and said:

"I acted mighty mean today, Becky, and I'm so sorry. I won't ever, ever do that way again. Please make up, won't you?"

The girl stopped and looked at him angrily.

"I'll thank you to keep yourself *to* yourself, Mr. Thomas Sawyer. I'll never speak to you again."

She tossed her head and left.

Poor girl, she did not know how she would regret her words that very day.

The teacher, Mr. Dobbins, had always wanted to be a doctor. He still took out a medical book every day and read it when the students were working. He kept the book locked up, and every child in the school wanted to see what was inside it. Now, as Becky was passing by the desk, she noticed that the drawer was open, unlocked! This was her chance. She reached in and pulled out the "secret" book. The title page (Professor Somebody's *Anatomy*) meant nothing to her, so she began to turn the pages. She came to a page that had a picture of a person—with no clothes on!

At that moment, Tom stepped in the door and saw her. Becky grabbed at the book to close it, and had the bad luck to tear the page right down the middle. She stuffed the book back into the desk and burst out crying with shame.

"Tom Sawyer, you are just as mean as you can be, to sneak up on me. You ought to be ashamed of yourself. You know you're going to tattle-tale on me, and oh, I'll be whipped, and I never was whipped in school."

Then she stamped her little foot and hurried to her desk.

A whole hour drifted by. And then it happened. Mr. Dobbins unlocked his desk and reached for his book. Tom shot a look at Becky. She looked helpless and scared. Tom forgot about his anger with her. Quick—something must be done to help her. He thought he could grab the book and fly out the door, but it was too late—the teacher was already turning the pages! There was no help for Becky now, he thought.

The teacher stood up, a look of anger in his eyes. "Who tore this book?" he shouted.

There was not a sound. Mr. Dobbins started questioning each child.

Soon Mr. Dobbins came to Becky Thatcher. Tom was trying to think what to do.

"Rebecca Thatcher!" (Tom glanced at her face—it was white with terror.) "Did you tear this book?"

A new idea shot like lightning through Tom's brain. He sprang to his feet and shouted:

"I done it!"

The loving looks of thanks in Becky's eyes made the whipping Tom got worthwhile. Becky met him after school and told him she was sorry for saying she'd never speak to him again. Tom forgave her, and fell asleep that night with Becky's last words ringing in his ears—

"Tom, how *could* you be so good and kind!"

Tom was happy, not only because of Becky, but also because school was just about done for the year, and summer vacation would soon begin.

CHAPTER TEN

The Murder Trial – Facing Injun Joe

School hadn't been out for long when Tom started to get a little bored. Becky had gone away to her summer home, and he was running out of things to do.

He tried keeping a diary, but nothing happened for three days, so he gave it up. The first of the traveling shows came to town. Tom and Joe Harper got up a band of performers and were happy for two days.

A circus came. The boys played circus for three days afterward in tents made of rag carpeting— ticket price was three pins for boys, two for girls— and then circusing was given up.

Just when Tom was running out of ideas, the sleepy summer became a lot more exciting when Muff Potter's murder trial began. It was the talk of the village. Tom could not get away from it. It kept him in a cold shiver all the time. He met alone with Huck to be sure he had said nothing about that awful night in the graveyard.

"Huck, have you ever told anybody about—that?"

"Oh—course I haven't. What makes you ask?"

"Well, I was scared."

"Why, Tom Sawyer, we wouldn't have been alive two days if we'd told. *You* know that."

Tom felt better.

"Huck, nobody could get you to tell, could they?"

"Get me to tell? Why would I tell and have Injun Joe kill me?"

"Well, that's all right, then. I reckon we're safe as long as we keep our mouths shut," said Tom.

"Me too. I reckon old Muff's a goner, though. I feel sorry for him, sometimes. He don't amount to much, but he ain't ever done anything to hurt anybody. Just fishes a little and loafs around a lot. But he's kind of good—he give me half a fish once."

"Well, he's fixed kites for me, Huck, and tied fishin' hooks to my line. I wish we could get him out of there, 'specially since he never done the murder."

As the twilight came, the boys went, as they had before, to the jail cell and gave Potter some treats. Muff was so thankful and kind to them that Tom felt more guilty than ever about keeping the secret.

For two days Tom hung around outside the courtroom. Things were looking very bad for Muff Potter. At the end of the second day, the talk was that Injun Joe's story about the killing would bring a guilty verdict from the jury the very next day. Tom wondered what he should do.

The whole village was at the courthouse the next morning. The jury came in and took their places. Shortly afterward, Potter was brought in with chains around him, and he was seated where Injun Joe could stare right at him. The judge and the lawyers arrived and began to call witnesses.

Every one of the witnesses swore to facts that made it sound as though Muff had done the killing. Muff's lawyer didn't even *bother* to question the witnesses! Nobody, including the judge, understood what Muff's lawyer might be up to. Finally, when it looked as though Muff was sure to be framed for the murder, his lawyer stood and began to speak.

"Your Honor, we said at the opening of this trial that we would prove that our client did this terrible thing in a moment of insanity while drunk. We have changed our mind. We are changing our plea to *not guilty!*" Turning to the clerk, he said, "Call Thomas Sawyer to the stand!"

The whole courtroom was shocked and puzzled, including Muff Potter. Every eye watched as Tom took a seat before the judge and swore to tell the truth.

"Thomas Sawyer, where were you on the seventeenth of June, about the hour of midnight?"

Tom glanced at Injun Joe's mean face, and his tongue wouldn't work. After a few moments, the boy got a little of his strength back, and answered weakly, "In the graveyard!"

A hateful smile flitted across Injun Joe's face.

"Were you near Hoss Williams's grave?"

"Yes, sir."

"Were you hidden, or not?"

"I was hid behind the elm trees that's on the edge of the grave."

Injun Joe sat up in his seat.

"Anyone with you?"

"Yes, sir. I went there with—"

"Wait—wait a moment. Never mind the other name. We will call him as a witness later. Did you carry anything there with you?"

Tom hesitated and looked confused.

"Speak out, my boy. The truth is always best. What did you take there?"

"Only a—a—dead cat."

There was a ripple of laughter, which the court put a stop to.

"We will produce the skeleton of that cat," smiled Muff's lawyer. "Now, my boy, tell us everything that happened—tell it in your own way—don't skip anything, and don't be afraid."

Tom began, and every eye was on him as the audience heard the terrible tale. Every person was on the edge of his seat as Tom said:

"—and as the doctor knocked Muff Potter down with the headboard, Injun Joe jumped with the knife and—"

Crash! Quick as lightning, Injun Joe sprang for a window, tore his way through all who tried to stop him, and was gone!

CHAPTER ELEVEN

A Hero–Digging for Hidden Treasure

Tom was a hero once more. The villagers were now as nice to Muff Potter as they had been mean to him before.

Tom's days were wonderful, but his nights were times of horror. Injun Joe was in all his dreams. Poor Huck was in the same state of terror when he found out Tom had told the whole story to the lawyer the night before the trial. Huck was afraid that *his* part in the thing might leak out. At least Injun Joe's escape had saved Huck from having to testify in court! But Huck had lost faith in people when Tom couldn't keep a secret—even after Tom and Huck had sworn their secret oath.

Rewards had been offered and the countryside was searched, but no Injun Joe was found. The days drifted on, and each day helped to take away a little of Tom's fear. He began to think of new ways to stay busy and have fun. He decided to do what every normal boy wants to do sometime in his life—dig for hidden treasure!

Tom found Huck and laid out his plans. Huck was always willing to try anything that sounded fun and required no money.

"Where'll we dig?" said Huck.

"Oh, most anywhere."

"Why, is it hid all around?"

"No, indeed it ain't. It's hid in mighty special places, Huck."

"Who hides it?"

"Why, robbers, of course—who'd you reckon? Sunday school teachers?"

"Don't they come after it anymore?"

"No, they *think* they will, but they generally forget the directions to it, or else they die. Anyway, it lays there a long time and gets rusty, and then somebody finds an old yellow paper that tells where to find it."

"Have you got one of them papers, Tom?"

"No."

"Well, then, how you going to find the clues?"

"I don't need any. They always bury it under a haunted house or on an island, or under a dead tree where the shadow of its one limb falls at midnight."

"Is it under all of them?"

"How you talk! No!"

"Then how you going to know which one to go for?"

"Go for all of 'em!"

"Why, Tom, it'll take all summer."

"Well, what of that? Suppose you find a rotten chest with a hundred dollars in it?"

"That's good enough for me! But say, where you going to dig first?"

"Well, I don't know. S'pose we try that old dead-limb tree on the hill t'other side of Still-House Creek?"

"I'm agreed."

So they got a broken pick-axe and a shovel, and began their three-mile hike. When they arrived, they threw themselves down in the shade of a tree to rest.

"I like this," said Tom.

"So do I."

"Say, Huck, if we find a treasure here, what you going to do with your share?"

"Well, I'll have pie and a glass of soda every day, and I'll go to every circus that comes along. What you going to do with your'n, Tom?"

"I'm going to buy a new drum, and a sure-'nuff sword, and a red necktie, and a dog, and get married."

"Married?"

"That's it."

"Tom, you—why, you ain't in your right mind."

"Wait—you'll see."

"What's the name of the gal?"

"It ain't a gal at all—it's a girl."

"It's all the same, I reckon. Some says gal, some says girl. Anyway, what's her name, Tom?"

"I'll tell you maybe—later on. Now forget about this and we'll go to digging."

They worked and sweated for half an hour. Nothing. They dug another half-hour. Still no luck.

Huck said, "Do they always bury it as deep as this?"

"Sometimes—not always. I reckon we haven't got the right place."

So they chose a new spot and began again. Finally Huck leaned on his pick-axe, wiped the sweat from his face and said:

"Where you going to dig next, after we get this one?"

"I reckon maybe we'll try the old tree that's over yonder on Cardiff Hill back of the Widow Douglas's mansion."

"I reckon that'll be a good one."

The work went on. After a while Huck said, "Dern it, we must be in the wrong place again. What do you think?"

"It is mighty strange, Huck, but I think I know what the matter is! What fools we are! You got to find out where the shadow of the limb falls at midnight, and *that's* where you dig!"

"Shucks! We've fooled away all this work for nothing. Now hang it all, we got to come back in the night. Can you get out?"

"You bet! We've got to do it tonight, too, because if somebody sees these holes they'll know in a minute what's here, and they'll go for it."

"Well, I'll come around and me-yow tonight."

"All right. Let's hide the tools in the bushes."

The boys were there that night somewhere around midnight. They marked where the shadow fell, and began to dig. The hole got deeper and deeper.

At last Tom said, "It ain't any use, Huck. We're wrong again."

"Well, but we *can't* be wrong. We spotted the shadow exactly."

"I know it, but then there's another thing."

"What's that?"

"Why, we only guessed at the time. Probably it wasn't dead-on midnight."

Huck dropped his shovel. "Say, Tom, let's give this place up, and try somewheres else."

"All right, I reckon we better. Let's try the haunted house."

"Dern it, I don't like haunted houses, Tom. Why, that's just where ghosts come sliding around and peep over your shoulder."

"Yes, but, Huck, ghosts only travel around at night. They won't stop us from digging there in the daytime."

"Well, that's so. We'll try that haunted house in the daytime if you say so, but I reckon it's taking chances."

They had started down the hill by this time. There in the middle of the moonlit valley below them stood the "haunted" house, all alone, weeds covering the doorsteps, the windows broken, a corner of the roof caved in. The boys stayed well away from it and went home through the woods on the rear side of Cardiff Hill.

CHAPTER TWELVE

Hiding Above – Gold Below

The next day the boys were heading toward the woods when they remembered it was Friday. It was bad luck to be fooling around with ghosts on a Friday, so they decided to play Robin Hood for the rest of the day. Lots of rich people were robbed, and lots of money given to the poor by a make-believe band of merry men.

On Saturday, shortly after noon, the boys picked up their tools at the dead tree and headed for the haunted house. They crept to the door and took a trembling peek, only to see a huge room full of hanging cobwebs. An old crumbling fireplace stood on one wall near a broken-down staircase.

Soon they were inside, talking in whispers.

In a little while, seeing no ghosts and getting braver, they threw their tools into a corner and went up the rickety old stairs. Finding nothing in an empty closet, they were about to go back downstairs and begin digging when—

"Sh!" said Tom.

"What is it?" whispered Huck, frightened.

"Sh! ... There! ... Hear it?"

"Yes! ... Oh, my! Let's run!"

"Keep still! Don't you move! They're coming right toward the door."

The boys stretched themselves out and looked through a hole in the floor, scared to death.

Two men entered.

Tom whispered, "There's the old deaf and dumb Spaniard that's been nosin' around town lately— never seen the other man before."

The "other man" was a ragged creature with a mean face. The Spaniard, wrapped in a colorful cape, had bushy white whiskers and long white hair that flowed from under his sombrero. The ragged man was speaking:

"No," he said, "I've thought it all over, and I don't like it. It's dangerous."

"Dangerous! Nonsense!" grunted the "deaf and dumb" Spaniard—to the surprise of the boys, because if he was deaf and dumb, how could he hear and talk?

The Spaniard's voice made the boys gasp and shake with fear. It was Injun Joe's!

"What's any more dangerous than that job up yonder?" he growled. "But nothing's come of it."

"That's different. It was way up the river with nobody around. It won't ever be known that we tried, anyway, since we didn't succeed."

"Well, what's more dangerous than coming here in the daytime?!—anybody would suspect us that saw us."

"I know that. But there warn't any other place as handy after that fool of a job. I want to get out of this house. I wanted to yesterday, only it warn't any use trying to stir out of here, with those boys playing over there on the hill right in front of us."

Tom and Huck shook again when they heard this, and thought how lucky it was that they had remembered it was Friday and decided to wait a day.

After a long silence Injun Joe said, "Look here, you go back up the river where you belong. Wait there till you hear from me. I'll take the chances on dropping into this town just once more, for a look. We'll do that 'dangerous' job after I've snooped around a little and think things look better for it. Then we'll get out of here and head for Texas. Now, I'm going to get some sleep! It's your turn to watch."

The "Spaniard" was soon snoring. It wasn't very long before the other man had also fallen asleep.

The boys drew a long, grateful breath. Tom whispered, "Now's our chance—come."

But just then, one snore stopped. Injun Joe sat up, looked around, and stirred his partner awake with his foot.

"Here, you're a fine watchman, ain't you! Nearly time for us to be moving, pard. What'll we do with the stolen loot we've got left?"

"I don't know—leave it here as we've always done, I reckon. No use to take it away till we start south. Six hundred and fifty in silver's a lot to carry."

Tom and Huck looked at each other with wide eyes and open mouths.

"Well—all right—it won't hurt to come here once more and get it," said Injun Joe.

"No—but I'd say come in the night as we used to do—it's better," said the partner.

"Yes, but it may be a good while before I get the right chance at that other job. Accidents might happen. It ain't in such a very good place. We better bury it—and bury it deep."

"Good idea," said the partner. He walked across the room, knelt down, raised one of the stones in the fireplace and took out a bag that jingled nicely. He passed the bag to Joe, who was on his knees, digging with his knife.

The boys forgot all their fears in an instant. With greedy eyes they watched every movement. Luck! Here was the best kind of treasure hunting—they would know right where to dig!

Then Joe's knife struck something.

"What is it?" said his partner.

"Half-rotten board—no, it's a box," Injun Joe replied.

He reached his hand in and drew it out—

"Man, it's money!"

The two men pulled out several gold coins. The boys above were just as excited as the men below.

"We'll make quick work of this," said the ragged partner. "There's an old rusty pick-axe over among the weeds in the corner."

He ran and grabbed the boys' pick-axe and shovel. Injun Joe took the pick-axe, looked it over, and began digging. The box was soon out of the ground. The men stared at the treasure.

"Pard, there's thousands of dollars here," said Injun Joe.

"It was always said that Murrel's gang used to hang around here one summer," the ragged man said.

"I know it," said Injun Joe, "and this looks like some of their old loot."

"*Now* you won't need to do that *other* job."

Injun Joe frowned.

"You don't know me. And you don't know all that's behind the reason for that other job. It ain't only robbery—it's *revenge!*" A wicked light flamed in his eyes. "I'll need your help in it. When it's finished—then Texas. Go home to your Nance and your kids, and stand by till you hear from me."

"Well—if you say so. What'll we do with this— bury it again?" said the partner.

"Yes. [*There was great delight overhead.*] No! [*There was great distress overhead.*] I'd nearly forgot. That pick-axe had fresh earth on it! [*The boys became sick with terror.*] Why would there be a pick and a shovel here with fresh dirt on them? Who brought them here—and where have they gone? Have you heard anybody?—seen anybody? What!—bury it again and leave them to come and see the ground dug up? Not a chance. We'll take it to my den," said Injun Joe.

"Why, of course! Might have thought of that before. You mean Number One?"

"No—Number Two—under the cross. The other place is bad—too common."

"All right. It's nearly dark enough to start."

They slipped out of the house in the twilight, and moved toward the river with their box of treasure.

Tom and Huck stood up, weak but thankful, and stared after them through the cracks between the logs of the house.

The two boys did not talk much as they made their way down the hill toward town. They were thinking what bad luck it was, leaving the shovel and the pick there. Except for that, Injun Joe would have hidden the silver with the gold right there until his "revenge job" was taken care of, and then he would have returned and found that the money was missing. Bad, bad luck that the tools were ever brought there!

They decided to keep a lookout for that "Spaniard" when he came to town looking for chances to do his "revenge job," and follow him to den "Number Two," wherever that might be. Then Tom had a horrible thought.

"Revenge? What if he means *us*, Huck?!"

"Oh, don't say that!" said Huck, nearly fainting.

They talked it all over and agreed to believe that Injun Joe might possibly mean somebody else—at least that he might mean nobody but Tom, since Tom was the only one of them that Injun Joe had seen at Muff Potter's trial.

It wasn't much comfort to Tom to be the only one in danger! Having a little company would be an improvement, he thought.

CHAPTER THIRTEEN

On Watch – In Room 2

After a quick breakfast the next morning, Tom went toward town and found Huck dangling his legs over a flatboat, looking forlorn.

"Hello, Huck! Why so sad?"

"Tom, if we'd-a left the dern tools at the dead tree, we'd-a got the money. Oh, ain't it awful!"

"Huck, we gotta track them to find that money."

"Tom, we'll never find Injun Joe. I'd feel mighty shaky if I was to see him, anyway."

"Well, so'd I, but I'd like to track him down to his Number Two hideout."

"Number Two—yes, that's it. I been thinkin' 'bout that. What do you reckon it is?"

"I dunno. Say, Huck—maybe it's the number of a house!"

"Goody! ... No, Tom, that ain't it. If it is, it ain't in this little town. Ain't no house numbers here."

"Well, that's so. Lemme think a minute. Maybe it's the number of a room—in a tavern, you know!"

"Oh, that's the trick! There ain't but two taverns. We can find out quick."

"You stay here, Huck, till I come back."

Tom was off at once. He found that, in the best tavern, Room 2 was rented by a young lawyer. In the other tavern, Room 2 was a mystery. The tavern-keeper's young son said it was kept locked all the time, and he never saw anybody go into it or come out of it, except at night. He said he had noticed that there was a light in there the night before. Tom rushed back and told Huck.

"That's what I've found out, Huck. I reckon that's the very Number Two we're after."

"I reckon it is, Tom. Now what you going to do?"

"I'll tell you. The back door of that Room Two is the door that comes out into that little alley between the tavern and the old brick store. Now, you get hold of all the door keys you can find, and I'll snitch all of Auntie's, and the first dark night

we'll go there and try 'em. And be sure you keep a lookout for Injun Joe, because he said he was going to drop into town and spy around once more for a chance to get his revenge. If you see him, you just follow him. If he don't go to that Room Two, that ain't the place."

"Lordy, I don't want to foller him by myself!"

"Why, it'll be night, sure. He might not ever see you—and if he did, maybe he'd never think anything."

"Well, if it's pretty dark I reckon I'll track him. I'll try."

"Now you're *talking!* Don't you ever weaken, Huck, and I won't."

Three nights later, Thursday, was the first dark night with no moon. An hour before midnight, the tavern closed up and its lights were put out. Nobody had entered or left the alley.

Tom got his lantern, and the two boys crept forward in the gloom. Huck stood watch and Tom felt his way toward the tavern. After what seemed like hours, there was a sudden flash of light, and Tom came tearing by him.

"Run!" he said. "Run for your life!"

The boys never stopped till they reached a shed at the lower end of the village. As soon as Tom got his breath he said:

"Huck, it was awful! I didn't need the keys. The door was unlocked and I walked right in! Then…"

"What!—what'd you see, Tom?"

"Huck, I 'most stepped onto Injun Joe's hand!"

"No!"

"Yes! He was lying there, sound asleep on the floor."

"Lordy, what did you do? Did he wake up?"

"No, never moved. Drunk, I reckon. I just got out of there!"

"Say, Tom, did you see that box?"

"Huck, I didn't wait to look around. I didn't see the box. I didn't see the cross. I didn't see anything but a bottle and a tin cup on the floor by Injun Joe, and a whole bunch more whiskey bottles around."

"Say, Tom, now's a mighty good time to get that box if Injun Joe's drunk."

"Right! *You* try it!"

Huck shuddered. "Well, no—I reckon not."

"And I reckon not, Huck. Lookyhere, let's not try that thing again till we know Injun Joe's not in there. It's too scary. Now, if we watch every night, we'll be dead sure to see him go out, some time or other, and then we'll snatch that box quicker'n lightning."

"Well, I'm agreed. I'll watch the whole night long every night if you'll do the other part of the job."

"All right, I will. All you got to do is to run up Hooper Street a block and me-yow—and if I'm asleep, you throw some gravel at the window and that'll get me up."

"Agreed!"

"Now, Huck, I'll go home. It'll begin to be daylight in a couple of hours. You go back and watch that long, will you?"

"I said I would, Tom, and I will. I'll sleep all day in Ben Rogers's hay barn, and I'll stand watch all night."

"Well, I won't need you in the daytime, Huck. I'll let you sleep. Whenever you see something's up during the night, just skip right around and me-yow."

CHAPTER FOURTEEN

McDougal's Cave – Huck the Spy

The first thing Tom heard on Friday morning was good news—Judge Thatcher's family had come back to town, and Becky had talked her mother into having the picnic the next day. Tom was so excited about the treasure and seeing Becky again he could barely sleep that night.

Morning came, and a happy group of children was gathered at Judge Thatcher's. Several young men and ladies went along as guardians. Soon the cheery crowd headed down Main Street toward the old steam ferryboat which had been rented for the day. Sid was sick and had to miss the fun. Cousin Mary remained at home to entertain him.

The last thing Mrs. Thatcher said to Becky was: "You'll not get back till late. Perhaps you'd better stay all night with some of the girls that live near the ferrylanding, child."

"Then I'll stay with Susy Harper, Mamma," Becky had said.

"Very well. And don't get into any trouble."

Three miles below town the ferryboat stopped. The crowd went ashore and the forest and hills were full of screams and laughter. After a picnic feast, somebody shouted:

"Who wants to explore McDougal's Cave?"

Everybody did! They all grabbed candles and headed up the hillside to a large cave with lots of underground rooms and tunnels. Most of the young men knew a part of it, but it was still easy to get turned around and lost in this dark, crooked cave. It was said that one might wander days and nights in its tangle of tunnels and pits and never find the end of it. Tom Sawyer knew as much of the cave as anyone.

Time flew by as the happy boys and girls chased each other around the tunnels of the cave. It was almost night when most of them returned to the boat.

Meanwhile, Huck was already on his watch. Eleven o'clock came and the tavern lights were put out. Huck waited what seemed a long time, but nothing happened.

Then he heard a noise. The next moment two men brushed by him, and one seemed to have something under his arm. It must be that box! So they were going to remove the treasure. Why call Tom now? It would be silly—the men would get away with the box and never be found again. No, he would follow them.

They moved through the streets and took the road past the old Welshman's house that led to the top of Cardiff Hill. There they disappeared into a narrow path, hidden by bushes. Huck got closer, afraid he had lost them. He was about to start running, when a man cleared his throat not four feet from him! Huck's heart shot into his throat, but he swallowed it again. He saw that he was within five steps of the stone wall entrance to Widow Douglas's place. *Very well*, he thought, *let them bury it there. It won't be hard to find*.

Now there was a voice—a very low voice—Injun Joe's: "Curse her, maybe she's got company! There's lights on."

A deadly chill went to Huck's heart—this must be the "revenge job"! His thought was to run away. Then he remembered that the Widow Douglas had been kind to him, and maybe these men were going to murder her. He wished he could go warn her, but he knew he didn't dare.

"Yes. Well, there *is* company there, I reckon. Better forget it, Joe," said the partner.

"Forget it, just when I'm getting out of this country forever? Forget it and maybe never have another chance? I tell you again, I don't care for her money—you may have it. But her husband was rough on me. He was the man that had me horsewhipped—with all the town looking on! *Horsewhipped!*—do you understand? *He's* dead now—but I'll take it out on *her*."

"Oh, don't kill her! Don't do that!"

"Kill? Who said anything about killing? I would kill *him* if he was here, but not her. When you want to get revenge on a woman you don't kill her—you go for her looks. You cut her face bad!"

"By God, that's awful!"

"If you don't help me with this, I'll kill you. Do you understand that? And if I have to kill you, I'll kill her—and then I reckon nobody will ever know who done this crime."

"Well, if it's got to be done, let's get at it. The quicker the better."

"Do it *now*, while company's there? No—we'll wait till the lights are out."

Huck backed away a few steps as quietly as he could. Then he turned and ran until he reached the Welshman's house. He banged at the door, and the heads of the old man and his two sons popped out of the windows.

"What's going on there? Who's banging? What do you want?" cried the Welshman.

"Let me in—quick! I'll tell everything."

"Why, who are you?"

"Huckleberry Finn—quick, let me in!"

"Huckleberry Finn! It ain't a name to open many doors, but let him in, lads, and let's see what's the trouble."

"Please don't ever tell I told you," were Huck's first words when he got in. "Please don't—I'd be killed, sure—but the Widow Douglas has been good friends to me sometimes, and I want to tell you."

"By George, he has got something to tell, or he wouldn't act so!" cried the old man. "Out with it, and nobody here will ever tell, lad."

Huck told all he had heard, and three minutes later the old man and his sons were up the hill, entering the bushes on tiptoe, their guns in their hands. Huck hid behind a big rock and listened. All of a sudden there was an explosion of guns and a cry.

Huck waited no longer. He jumped up and ran down the hill as fast as his legs could carry him.

CHAPTER FIFTEEN

A Widow Is Saved–A Cave Is Searched

As soon as the sun came up on Sunday, Huck went back up the hill and rapped at the Welshman's door.

"Who's there?"

"Please let me in! It's only Huck Finn!"

"It's a name that can open this door, night or day—and welcome," said the Welshman. "Now, my boy, I hope you're good and hungry, because breakfast will be ready soon. I and the boys hoped you'd come back here last night."

"I was awful scared," said Huck, "and I ran when the pistols went off. I've come now becuz I wanted to know what happened. Are those devils dead?"

"No, they ain't dead. Just as we sneaked up on them, I sneezed—and they took off running. We fired some shots and they fired back, but we didn't catch them. The Sheriff, his men, and my boys will search the woods this morning. I wish we knew what those rascals looked like. But you couldn't see what they looked like in the dark, could you?"

"Oh, yes. I saw them in town and followed 'em."

"Good! Describe them—describe them, my boy!"

"One's the old deaf and dumb Spaniard that's been hanging around here, and the other's a mean-looking, ragged—"

"That's enough, lad, we know the men! Happened to see them in the woods back of the widow's one day, and they sneaked away. Get going, boys, and tell the Sheriff."

The Welshman's sons left at once. As they were leaving the room, Huck jumped up, shouting:

"Oh, please don't tell anybody it was me that told on them!"

"All right if you say so, Huck, but you ought to get the credit for what you did."

"Oh, no, no! Please don't tell!"

When the young men were gone, the old Welshman said, "They won't tell—and I won't.

But why don't you want it known?"

Huck would not explain, except to say that he would be killed if the men thought he knew anything about them.

"How did you come to follow these men?" asked the Welshman. "Were they acting strange?"

Huck didn't want to tell the whole story, so he said he just happened to wake up around midnight and go out walking, and that he noticed the deaf and dumb Spaniard and his ragged partner, and thought they might be robbers.

"Then they went on," said the Welshman, "and you followed 'em?"

"Followed 'em—yes. That was it. I tracked 'em to the widow's gate and stood in the dark and heard the ragged man beg for the widow's life, and the Spaniard swear he'd spoil her looks just as I told you and your two—"

"What?! The *deaf and dumb* man said all that? How could he talk?"

Huck was caught! He was trying his best to keep the old man from knowing who the Spaniard might be, but he kept making mistakes in his story. The Welshman knew that Huck was not telling him the whole story. He put his hand on Huck's shoulder.

"My boy, don't be afraid of me. This Spaniard is not deaf and dumb. He *can* hear and he *can* talk. You've let that slip out without meaning to, and you can't cover that up now. You know something about that Spaniard that you want to keep hidden. Now, trust me—tell me what it is, and trust ol' Jones—I won't let you get in trouble."

Huck looked into the old man's honest eyes a moment, then bent over and whispered in his ear:

"It ain't a Spaniard—it's Injun Joe!"

Mr. Jones almost jumped out of his chair.

"That sounds exactly like something Injun Joe would do. Now come, my boy, and have something to eat. You look very sickly."

During breakfast the talk went on. Huck didn't say a thing about the treasure. And he was pretty sure the Welshman hadn't found it, because he had said that all he and his boys had come across was a bag of robber's tools. Huck figured that the treasure must still be in Room 2. The men would be caught and jailed, and he and Tom could go get the gold that night.

Just after breakfast, there was a knock at the door. Huck jumped for a hiding place. Several people came in, among them the Widow Douglas. The Welshman told the story to the visitors. The widow went on and on thanking him for his help.

"Don't say a word about it, madam. There's someone else to be thanked more than me, but he don't allow me to tell his name. We wouldn't have been there if it weren't for him."

Everybody at church that morning was talking about the news of the night before. When the sermon was finished, Judge Thatcher's wife walked out with Mrs. Harper.

"Is my Becky going to sleep all day?" she said to Mrs. Harper.

"Your Becky?"

"Yes!" Mrs. Thatcher had a startled look. "Didn't she stay with you last night?"

"Why, no."

Mrs. Thatcher turned pale and sat down, just as Aunt Polly passed by.

"Good morning, Mrs. Thatcher," said Aunt Polly. "Good morning, Mrs. Harper. I've got a boy that's turned up missing. I reckon my Tom stayed at one of your houses last night. And now he's afraid to come to church."

Mrs. Thatcher shook her head sadly and turned whiter than ever.

"He didn't stay with us," said Mrs. Harper, looking upset as her son, Joe, walked over.

"Joe Harper, have you seen my Tom this morning?" Aunt Polly asked worriedly.

"No, ma'am."

"When did you see him last?"

Joe couldn't say for sure. The other children said they didn't remember seeing Tom and Becky get on the ferryboat. It had been dark and nobody had thought much about it. One young man finally said he was afraid that they were still in the cave! Mrs. Thatcher fainted. Aunt Polly began crying.

The alarm went out and the whole village started a search. Soon, two hundred men were heading toward the cave. All night, Mrs. Thatcher, Aunt Polly, and the town waited for news, but when morning dawned all the word that came was: "Send more candles—and send food."

The old Welshman came home toward daylight the next morning, worn out from helping to search the cave. He found Huck still in bed, sick with fever. The doctors were all at the cave, so the Widow Douglas came to stay with Huck.

The search dragged on for three awful days and nights. Men searched the tunnels, calling out for Tom and Becky and firing pistol shots. In a far part of the cave, the words "Becky and Tom" had been found traced upon the rocky wall in candle smoke. Nearby lay a piece of Becky's ribbon. Mrs. Thatcher cried that this would be the last memento of Becky she would ever have.

Huck stayed in a feverish sleep for days. During one wakeful moment he asked the Widow Douglas if Tom had been to see him. The old woman just said, "Hush, child," and began to cry.

Huck didn't know what to think of that, but fell back into a deep sleep.

CHAPTER SIXTEEN

Lost! – A Light in the Darkness

Now to return to Tom and Becky and their day at the picnic. They had explored all the side tunnels of the cave, lighting candles as things got darker and darker. Bats squeaked and flew into their faces. Water dripped onto their heads from the top of the cave. Before long, they were squeezing through very narrow tunnels. Tom wanted to show Becky all he knew, or *thought* he knew, about this mysterious world. On one wall they wrote their names using candle smoke. After some time, they came to an underground lake and sat down to rest. Now, for the first time, they realized how still and quiet it was.

"Why, I didn't notice," said Becky, "but it seems a long time since I heard any of the others. I wonder how long we've been down here, Tom. We better start back."

"Yes, I reckon we better."

"Can you find the way, Tom? It's all a mixed-up crookedness to me."

"I reckon I could find it. But let's not go by the bats again. If they put our candles out, it will be an awful mess. Let's try some other way."

They went through a tunnel, but everything looked strange to Tom. He began to think they were lost. Becky clung to his side in fear and started to cry.

Tom began shouting, hoping someone would hear him. The children stood still and listened, but there was no reply. Tom turned back the way they had come, but could not be sure which turns they had taken. Soon Becky knew that Tom could not find his way back.

"Tom, Tom, we're lost! We're lost! We never can get out of this awful place! Oh, why did we ever leave the others?"

She sank to the ground, crying. Tom put his arms around her to comfort her, and they went on again.

Tom blew out Becky's candle. They only had a few left and had to save them. Becky knew what this meant, and she lost hope.

They grew more and more tired until, at last Becky had to sit down. Tom rested with her, and they talked of home and their friends. Becky cried, and Tom tried to think of some way to help her. Before too long, she had fallen asleep.

When Becky woke up, they wandered along some more, hand in hand. A long time after this they came to a spring, and Tom said it was time to rest again. Tom fastened his candle to the wall in front of them with a bit of clay. Nothing was said for some time. Then Becky broke the silence:

"Tom, I am so hungry!"

Tom took a small piece of cake from his pocket, saved from the picnic. They both agreed it could be their "wedding cake." It would give them something to dream about. It tasted so good that Becky wanted to move on again, but Tom looked seriously into her eyes.

"Becky, can you stand it if I tell you something?"

Becky's face went white, but she nodded yes.

"Well… Becky, we must stay here where there's water. That little piece of wax is our last candle!"

"Tom!" Becky sobbed. "Won't they miss us and hunt for us?"

"Yes, they will! Certainly they will!"

"When would they miss us, Tom?"

"When they get back to the boat, I reckon."

"Tom, it might be dark then—would they notice we haven't come back?"

"I don't know. But anyway, your mother will miss you as soon as they get home."

Then they both remembered that Becky's mother had not expected her home that night. It could have been as late as Sunday noon before Mrs. Thatcher found out that Becky was not at Mrs. Harper's house.

The children watched the small bit of candle melt slowly away. The flame grew weaker, and then... everything was total darkness.

Time dragged on. They slept again, and awoke starving and sad. Tom believed it must be Tuesday by this time.

Then he had an idea. There were some side tunnels nearby. It would be better to search than do nothing at all.

He took a kite line from his pocket, tied it to a spot on the cave wall, and he and Becky started out, unwinding the line as they crawled along. At the end of twenty steps he came to what felt like a cliff or a jumping-off place. Tom got down on his knees and felt below and as far around the corner to the right as he could reach. At that moment, not twenty yards away, a human hand, holding a candle, appeared from behind a rock! Tom lifted up a happy shout, but instantly that hand was followed by the body it belonged to—Injun Joe's!

Tom was frozen with fear. He was most happy to see Injun Joe turn and run out of sight. He did not tell Becky what it was he had seen. He told her he had only shouted "for luck."

But fear gave way to hunger. After another long sleep, Tom thought that it must be Wednesday or Thursday or even Friday or Saturday now, and that the search had been given up. He decided to explore another tunnel. He felt willing to risk Injun Joe and all other terrors to find a way out.

But Becky was very weak. She said she would wait where she was, and die. With a lump in his throat, Tom kissed her cheek and tried to act brave. Then he took the kite line in his hand and went crawling down one of the tunnels, full of fear of the unknown.

Tuesday evening came, and the village of St. Petersburg still cried for its lost children. Most of the searchers had given up. The village went to bed on Tuesday night feeling hopeless.

Sometime in the middle of the night, village church bells began ringing. In a moment the streets were filled with people shouting, "They're found!

They're found!" Tin pans rang and horns blew as the people marched together toward the river. At last they were met by the children being drawn in a carriage. The villagers shouted hurrah after hurrah! It was the greatest night the little town had ever seen.

Tom lay on a sofa, telling the story of the wonderful adventure (adding a few extra things to make it more exciting). He told of how he left Becky to find a way out of the cave, following two paths as far as his kite line would reach. And how he followed a third and was about to turn back when he spotted a far-off speck of daylight. He told how he dropped the line, pushed his head and shoulders through a small hole, and saw the broad Mississippi River rolling by! He was proud to say that he had comforted Becky and kept her from dying, and had helped her find her way out. Then he told of how some men came along, gave them some food, and brought them home.

Three days and nights of hunger in the cave had been hard on Tom and Becky. They stayed in bed all day Wednesday and all of Thursday.

Tom got around town a little by Friday, but Becky
did not leave her room until Sunday.

Tom learned of
Huck's sickness,
but was not
allowed to see
him until Monday.
He saw Huck each
day at the widow's
house after that,
but was warned
to keep still about
his adventure in the cave
and to say nothing that would excite Huck.
At home, Tom learned what had
happened on Cardiff Hill and also
that Injun Joe's partner had been
found dead in the river, near
the ferrylanding. It
was thought he had
drowned while
trying to
escape.

About two weeks after Tom's rescue from the cave, he started off one morning to visit Huck, who was now strong enough to hear exciting talk—and Tom thought he had some that would interest him. Judge Thatcher's house was on Tom's way, so he stopped to see Becky. While he was there, he told Judge Thatcher that he wouldn't mind going back into the cave.

"Well, there are others just like you, I'm sure," said the Judge. "But we have taken care of that. Nobody will ever get lost in that cave again."

"Why?" asked Tom.

"Because I had its big door shut and sealed with iron and triple-locks—and I've got the keys."

Tom turned as white as a sheet.

"What's the matter, boy? Out with it! What is it?"

"Oh, Judge, Injun Joe's in the cave!"

CHAPTER SEVENTEEN

Return to the Cave—Under the Cross

Within a few minutes the news had spread, and boatloads of men were on their way to the cave. Tom Sawyer was in a boat with Judge Thatcher.

The cave door was unlocked and opened to a terrible sight! Injun Joe lay stretched upon the ground, dead. His face was close to the crack of the door and his Bowie knife was in his hand.

Tom felt sorry for him, for he knew how the man must have suffered. But Tom also felt a great relief, for he no longer had live in fear of this man.

Injun Joe was buried near the mouth of the cave. The villagers decided they were as happy with the funeral as they would have been with a hanging.

The morning after the funeral, Tom and Huck had a private talk. Huck had learned all about Tom's adventure from the Welshman and the Widow Douglas, but Tom told him there was one thing he *didn't* know. Before Tom could begin, Huck told about following Injun Joe on the night of the picnic.

"You followed him?" said Tom.

"Yes. If it hadn't been for me he'd be down in Texas by now."

Then Huck told *his* whole story in secret to Tom, who had only heard the Welshman's part of it before.

"And," said Huck, "I found out that Injun Joe wasn't carryin' the treasure that night. So, by now, somebody's sure searched that room and found the money. Anyways, I reckon we're out of luck, Tom. We'll never see that gold."

"Huck, that money wasn't ever in that Room Number Two!"

"What?! Tom, have you got on the track of that money again?"

"Huck, it's in the cave!"

Huck's eyes blazed.

"Say it again, Tom."

"The money's in the cave—it never was in the room in the tavern. That was just a place where Injun Joe went to find some whiskey. It was just plain, dumb luck that we happened to search for him there, thinking we should look for a room number. The *cave* was den Number Two all along."

"Tom—honest now—are you kiddin' me?"

"Honest, Huck—just as honest as ever I was in my life. Will you go in there with me and help get the money out?"

"You bet I will! I will if it's where we can find our way to it and not get lost."

"Huck, we can do that without the least little bit of trouble in the world."

"Good enough! What makes you think the money's—"

"Huck, you just wait till we get in there. If we don't find it, I'll agree to give you my drum and everything I've got in the world, by golly."

"All right—it's a deal. When do we go?"

"Right now, if you're strong enough."

"Is it far in the cave? I can't walk more'n a mile, Tom."

"It's about five mile into there the way anybody but me would go, Huck, but I know a shortcut. I'll take you right to it in a boat."

"Let's start right off, Tom."

"All right. We need some food, and a bag or two, and two or three kite strings, and some matches."

A little after noon, the boys "borrowed" a small boat from someone who was not at home. Several miles below Cave Hollow, Tom pointed out a white place on the hill that he had memorized as a landmark, and the boys went ashore.

"Now, Huck, where we're standing you could touch with a fishing pole that hole I got out of. See if you can find it."

Huck searched all over and found nothing. Tom proudly marched into a thick clump of bushes.

"Here you are! Look at it, Huck. It's the snuggest hole in the county. You just keep mum about it, though. This'll be the perfect place for us when we become robbers! We'll let Joe Harper and Ben Rogers in—because of course there's got to be a gang, or else there wouldn't be any style about it. Tom Sawyer's Gang—it sounds splendid, don't it, Huck?"

"Why, it's real bully, Tom. I believe it's better'n bein' a pirate."

The boys entered the hole, tying kite strings as they went so they could find their way back out. They passed the spring and went on until they reached the "jumping-off place." The candles showed that it was not really a cliff, but only a steep clay hill twenty or thirty feet high.

Tom whispered, "Now I'll show you something, Huck."

Holding his candle up, he said, "Look as far around the corner as you can. Do you see that mark over there on that big rock?"

"Tom, it's a *cross!*"

"*Now* where's your den Number Two? '*Under the cross,*' hey? Right there's where I saw Injun Joe holdin' up his candle, Huck!"

The boys hunted all over. They found some food scraps and blankets that must have been Injun Joe's, but there was no money box.

Finally, they decided it must be under the large rock that had the sign of the cross. Tom began digging under the rock with his knife and soon struck wood.

"Hey, Huck!—you hear that?"

Huck began to dig and scratch now. Some boards were uncovered and removed. Beneath the boards was a small tunnel under the rock. The boys slid into it, holding their candles to light the way. All at once Tom stopped.

"My goodness, Huck, lookyhere!"

It was the treasure box! Along with it were a couple of knives, a belt, and two or three pairs of old moccasins.

"Got it at last!" said Huck, running his hands through the gold coins. "My, but we're rich, Tom!"

"Huck, I always reckoned we'd get it. It's just too good to believe, but we *have* got it, sure! Say—let's not fool around here. Let's snake it out. Lemme see if I can lift the box."

Tom could lift the box but couldn't carry it.

"I thought so," he said. "I reckon I was right to bring the bags along."

The money was soon in the bags, and before long the boys were back in the boat eating their lunch. As the sun began to set, they pushed off and landed just after dark.

"Now, Huck," said Tom, "we'll hide the money in the room above the widow's woodshed. I'll come up in the morning and we'll count it and split it between us, and then we'll hunt up a place out in the woods for it where it will be safe. Just you lay quiet here and watch the stuff till I run and get Benny Taylor's little wagon."

When Tom returned with the wagon, the boys put the two sacks into it, threw some old rags on top, and started off. As they were passing the Welshman's house, Mr. Jones stepped out of the door and said, "Hallo, who's that?"

"Huck! And Tom Sawyer."

"Good! Come along with me, boys. You are keeping everybody waiting. Here, I'll haul the wagon for you. Why, it's pretty heavy. Got bricks in it?—or old metal?"

"Old metal," said Tom, thinking quickly.

"I thought so. The boys in this town will take more trouble and fool away more time hunting a little old iron to sell. But—hurry along inside, now!"

Soon Huck and Tom found themselves in Mrs. Douglas's parlor. Mr. Jones left the wagon near the door and followed them in. The place was all lit up, and there stood Tom's family and all the important people of the village, dressed in fancy clothes.

"Tom wasn't at home yet, so I gave him up," said the Welshman. "But I stumbled on him and Huck right at my door, and so I just brought them along in a hurry."

"And you did just right," said the widow. "Come with me, boys."

She took them to a bedroom and said, "Now wash and dress yourselves. Here are two new suits of clothes—shirts, socks, everything complete. Get into them and come down when you're cleaned up enough." Then she left.

CHAPTER EIGHTEEN

Riches–Rules–Rags–Robbers

Huck said, "Tom, we can slide out of here if we can find a rope. The window ain't high up."

"Shucks! What do you want to run away for?"

"Well, I ain't used to that kind of a crowd. I can't stand it. I ain't going down there, Tom."

"Oh, bother! It ain't anything. I don't mind it a bit. I'll take care of you."

Some minutes later, the widow's guests were at the supper table. Mr. Jones made a short speech, in which he thanked the widow for having the dinner honoring him and his two sons for protecting her. Then he sprung the secret about how Huck had been the *real* hero in helping to save the widow.

The widow showed her surprise at this and piled thanks after thanks on Huck, who was mighty uncomfortable being the center of attention.

The widow said she was going to give Huck a home under her roof and send him to school, and that when she could spare the money, she would start him in business.

Tom saw his chance and spoke up:

"Huck don't need it. Huck's rich. Huck's got money. Oh, you needn't smile—I reckon I can show you. You just wait a minute."

Tom ran out the door. The company looked at each other and at Huck, who was too tongue-tied to speak. Tom returned with the sacks, and poured all the coins on the table.

"There," he said. "Half of it's Huck's, and half of it's mine!"

Everyone was shocked and speechless for a minute. Then they all wanted an explanation. Tom said he could give it, and told the whole story.

The money was counted, and the sum came to over twelve thousand dollars. It was more cash than anyone there had ever seen at one time before.

The boys' money was the talk of St. Petersburg. Everyone began to say nice things about Huck and Tom. The village paper even printed stories about them.

The Widow Douglas put Huck's money in the bank to earn six percent interest, and Judge Thatcher did the same with Tom's, at Aunt Polly's request. Each boy had all the money he needed—a dollar a day from the interest!

Judge Thatcher came to think a lot of Tom. He said that no common boy would ever have got his daughter out of the cave, and that he hoped to see Tom become a great lawyer or a great soldier some day.

Because Huck Finn was now rich and under the Widow Douglas's care, he was dragged into society—and his pain was almost more than he could stand. The widow's servants kept him clean and neat, and they made him sleep in clean white sheets. He had to eat with a knife and fork and use a napkin, cup, and plate. He had to learn his books and go to church. And he had to speak just right.

He put up with this new way of life for three weeks, and then ran away.

Early one morning, after Huck had been missing for three days, Tom Sawyer found Huck just where he thought he would—in among some large, empty barrels. He was dirty, messy, and dressed in his old rags. Tom told him the trouble his disappearance had been causing, and begged him to go home. Huck's face looked sad.

"Don't talk about it, Tom. I've tried it, and it don't work. Tom, it ain't for me. I ain't used to it. The widow is good to me, and friendly, but I can't stand them ways. She makes me wash, and they comb me all to thunder. I got to wear them awful clothes, and go to church. I can't spit. I got to wear shoes all Sunday. I can't take it any more, Tom."

"Well, everybody does that way, Huck."

"Tom, I ain't everybody, and I can't *stand* it. It's awful to be tied up so. I got to ask to go a-fishing. I got to ask to go in a-swimming. Widow Douglas wouldn't let me yell, nor scratch in front of people. And besides that, school's going to open, and I'd-a had to go to it. Lookyhere, Tom, bein' rich ain't what it's cracked up to be. I wouldn't ever got into all this trouble if it hadn't-a been for that money. Now you just take my share of it and gimme a dime sometimes—not many times, becuz I don't give a dern for a thing unless it's hard to git—and you go tell the widow and get me out of this mess."

"Oh, Huck, you know I can't do that. 'Tain't fair. And besides, if you'll try this thing just a while longer, you'll come to like it."

"Like it! Yes—the way I'd like a hot stove if I was to set on it long enough. No, Tom, I like the woods and the river and sleepin' in empty barrels. Dern it all! Just as we'd found a secret hideout in a cave and could've become robbers, this foolishness has got to come up and spoil it all!"

Tom saw his chance. "Lookyhere, Huck, being rich ain't going to keep *me* from turning robber."

"No! Are you bein' honest, Tom?"

"Just as dead honest as I'm sitting here. But, Huck, we can't let you into the gang if you ain't respectable, you know."

Huck's joy left him. "Can't let me in, Tom? Didn't you let me be a pirate?"

"Yes, but that's different. A robber is more high-class than what a pirate is—usually."

"Now, Tom, hain't you always been friendly to me? You wouldn't leave me out, *would* you, Tom?"

"Huck, I wouldn't want to, and I *don't* want to— but what would people say? Why, they'd say Tom Sawyer's Gang had pretty low characters in it! They'd mean *you*, Huck. You wouldn't like that, and I wouldn't."

Huck was silent for some time. Finally he said, "Well, I'll go back to Widow Douglas for a month and see if I can learn to stand it, if you'll let me b'long to the gang, Tom."

"All right, Huck, it's a deal! Come along, and I'll ask the widow to let up on you a little."

"Will you, Tom—now, will you? When you going to start the gang and turn robbers?"

"Oh, right away. We'll get the boys together and have the swearing-in tonight, maybe."

"Have the which?"

"The swearing-in."

"What's that?"

"It's to swear to stand by one another, and never tell the gang's secrets, even if you're chopped all to bits."

"That sounds great, Tom, I tell you!"

"Well, I bet it is. And all that swearing's got to be done at midnight, in the lonesomest, awfulest place you can find—a haunted house is the best."

"Well, midnight's good, anyway, Tom."

"Yes, so it is. And you've got to swear on a coffin, and sign it with blood."

"Now, that's the life! Why, it's a million times better than pirating. I'll stick to the widow till I rot, Tom, and if I git to be a reg'lar ripper of a robber, with everybody talking 'bout it, I reckon she'll be proud she snaked me in out of the wet."

Conclusion

So ends this story. It being a history of a boy, it must stop here. The story could not go much further without becoming the history of a man. When one writes a novel about grown people, he knows exactly where to stop—that is, with a marriage. But when he writes of youngsters, he must stop where he best can.

Most of the characters that perform in this book are still living, and they are happy. Some day it may seem worthwhile to take up the story of the younger ones again and see what sort of men and women they turned out to be. Therefore, it will be wisest not to reveal any of that part of their lives at present.

MARK TWAIN

Mark Twain's real name was Samuel Langhorne Clemens. He was born in 1835, the year Halley's Comet blazed through the sky. He grew up in Hannibal, Missouri, where he rafted on the river and had an adventurous young life.

When his father died, young Samuel went to work as a typesetter for a newspaper. He traveled across America working as a typesetter, but he also held a variety of other jobs—from miner to soldier to riverboat pilot.

His own love of words and storytelling led him to become a writer. He took his pen name, Mark Twain, from a riverboat term which meant "two fathoms deep." His witty stories became very popular. In 1876, *The Adventures of Tom Sawyer* was published, which introduced America (and the world) to Tom Sawyer and Huck Finn. In 1885, *The Adventures of Huckleberry Finn* was another huge success. Mark Twain wrote several famous stories, including *The Prince and the Pauper* (1882) and *A Connecticut Yankee in King Arthur's Court* (1889).

Twain died in 1910, the same year Halley's Comet blazed again through the sky.